CW00644585

Contents

*C = copper; B = bronze

Each piece can be played either on E flat saxophones or on B flat saxophones.

Wet Dog

Mark Goddard

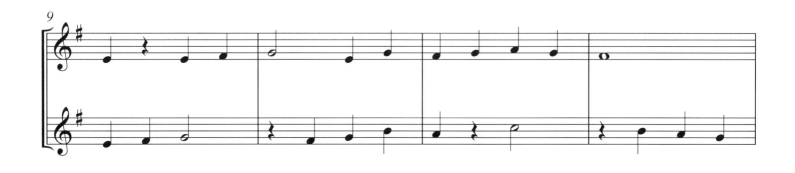

© 2005 by The Associated Board of the Royal Schools of Music

AB 3138

Earth Mover

James Rae

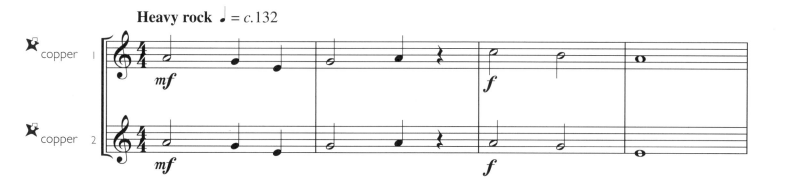

© 2005 by The Associated Board of the Royal Schools of Music

Cheer Leaders

Colin Cowles

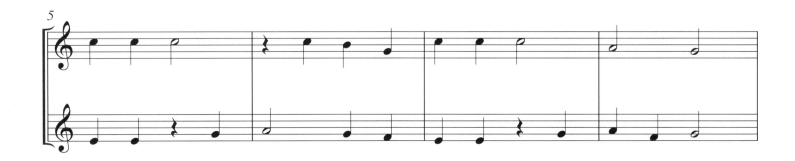

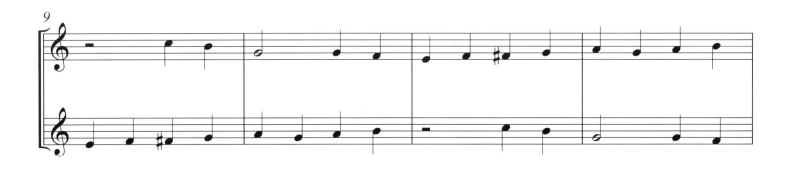

© 2005 by The Associated Board of the Royal Schools of Music

AB 3138

Team Tactics

Alan Bullard

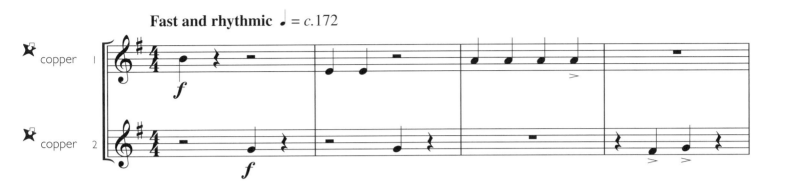

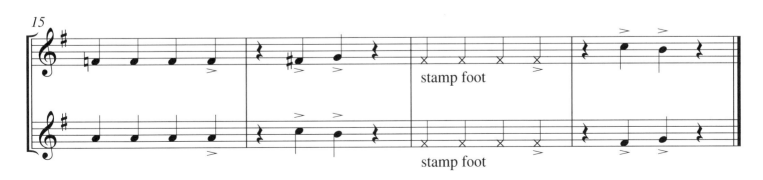

© 2005 by The Associated Board of the Royal Schools of Music

Blackberry and Apple Crumble

Paul Harris

© 2004 by The Associated Board of the Royal Schools of Music
This version © 2005 by The Associated Board of the Royal Schools of Music

AB 3138

Sweet as a Nut

Gordon Lewin

© 2005 by The Associated Board of the Royal Schools of Music

West Bay Rumba

James Rae

© 2005 by The Associated Board of the Royal Schools of Music

AB 3138

Theme from Symphony No. 9

Beethoven arr. Mark Goddard

© 2004 by The Associated Board of the Royal Schools of Music
This version © 2005 by The Associated Board of the Royal Schools of Music

No Time like the Present

Robert Tucker

© 2005 by The Associated Board of the Royal Schools of Music

AB 3138

Waltz in Blue

Mike Hall

© 2005 by The Associated Board of the Royal Schools of Music

Festival Fanfare

Alan Bullard

© 2005 by The Associated Board of the Royal Schools of Music

AB 3138

Show Time

Colin Cowles

© 2005 by The Associated Board of the Royal Schools of Music

AB 3138

The Carrion Crow

Trad. English arr. Gordon Lewin

© 2005 by The Associated Board of the Royal Schools of Music

14

AB 3138

Told by Bells

Gordon Lewin

© 2005 by The Associated Board of the Royal Schools of Music